This Little Tiger book belongs to:

_____

_____

_____

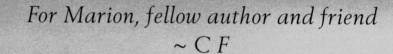

For Marion, fellow author and friend
~ C F

For my nephew, Jamie Wernert
~ T M

LITTLE TIGER PRESS LTD,
an imprint of the Little Tiger Group
1 Coda Studios, 189 Munster Road, London SW6 6AW
www.littletiger.co.uk
First published in Great Britain 2005
This edition published 2018
Text copyright © Claire Freedman 2004 • Illustrations copyright © Tina Macnaughton 2004
Claire Freedman and Tina Macnaughton have asserted their rights
to be identified as the author and illustrator of this work
under the Copyright, Designs and Patents Act, 1988
A CIP catalogue record for this book is available from the British Library

CD contains:
CD tracks 1-3 - complete story with original music and sound effects, plus lullaby
CD tracks 4-5 - story with page turn pings to encourage learner readers to join in

Running time over 17 mins
Produced by The Complete Works, Warwickshire CV31 1JP, in conjunction with Stationhouse
Music composed by Jim Betteridge and Sam Park
Story read by Lesley Sharp
This recording copyright © Little Tiger Press Ltd 2008
℗ Jim Betteridge and Sam Park

ISBN 978-1-78881-076-0
LTP/2700/2946/0719
Printed in China
10 9 8 7 6 5 4 3 2

Snuggle Up, Sleepy Ones

Claire Freedman   Tina Macnaughton

LITTLE TIGER

LONDON

The sun paints the sky
a warm, glowing red.
It's time to stop playing,
it's time for bed.

In the soft swampy mud
baby hippo, so snug,
Cuddles up close
for a big hippo hug.

Through wild, waving grasses
shy antelope roam.

It's been a long day,
they're ready for home.

Bold leopard cubs rest
from practising roars.
They snuggle together,
all tired, tangled paws.

Whilst up in the treetops
birds twitter and cheep,

Till quieter and quieter,
they fall fast asleep.

Below in their nests
baby porcupines all
Curl up, so snug tight,
in one spiky ball.

With tired, drooping necks
giraffe flop to the ground.
Sheltered and watched over.
Safe and sound.

And mischievous monkeys
shout down from the trees,
"It's not really dark yet.
Five more minutes, please!"

Zebras lay panting,
tired out from their play.
They sink into sleep
as the sun slips away.

Moths come a-fluttering,
bats flitter by.
Elephants rumble
their deep lullaby.

Shadows grow deeper,
the lion cubs doze.
Drowsy heads nod,
little eyes start to close.

Stars twinkle brightly,
the moon softly gleams.
Snuggle up, sleepy ones.
Hush now, sweet dreams!

More fabulous books from Little Tiger Press!

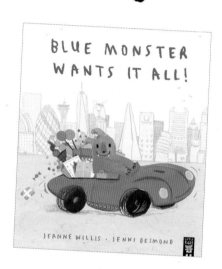

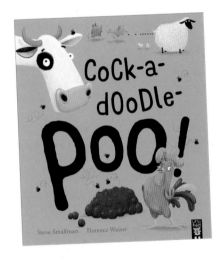

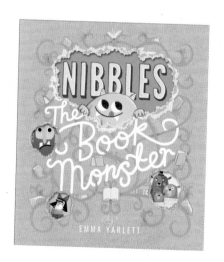

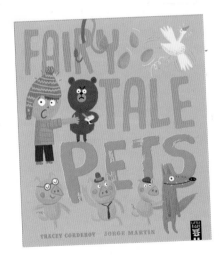

For information regarding any of the above books or for our catalogue, please contact us:
Little Tiger Press Ltd, 1 Coda Studios, 189 Munster Road, London SW6 6AW
Tel: 020 7385 6333 • E-mail: contact@littletiger.co.uk • www.littletiger.co.uk